Tree Frogs

by Helen Frost

spotted tree frog

Consulting Editor: Gail Saunders-Smith, Ph.D.

Consultant: Kevin Wright, D.V.M.
Curator of Ectotherms, Phoenix Zoo

Pebble Books

an imprint of Capstone Press
Mankato, Minnesota

Pebble Books are published by Capstone Press
151 Good Counsel Drive, P.O. Box 669, Mankato, Minnesota 56002
www.capstonepress.com

1 2 3 4 5 6 07 06 05 04 03 02

Library of Congress Cataloging-in-Publication Data
Frost, Helen, 1949–
    Tree frogs/by Helen Frost
    p. cm—(Rain forest animals)
    Includes bibliographical references (p. 23) and index.
    Summary: Simple text and photographs from the rain forest present the
characteristics and behavior of tree frogs.
    ISBN-13: 978-0-7368-1196-5 (hardcover)
    ISBN-10: 0-7368-1196-6 (hardcover)
    ISBN 13: 978-0-7368-9610-8 (softcover pbk.)
    ISBN 10: 0-7368-9610-4 (softcover pbk.)
    1. Hylidae—Juvenile literature. [1. Tree frogs. 2. Frogs.] I. Title.
QL668 .E24 F67 2002
597.8'78—dc21   2001003107

Note to Parents and Teachers

The Rain Forest Animals series supports national science standards
related to life science. This book describes and illustrates tree frogs
living in the rain forest. The photographs support early readers in
understanding the text. The repetition of words and phrases helps
early readers learn new words. This book also introduces early
readers to subject-specific vocabulary words, which are defined
in the Words to Know section. Early readers may need assistance
to read some words and to use the Table of Contents, Words to
Know, Read More, Internet Sites, and Index/Word List sections
of the book.

Table of Contents

4

Tree frogs
are amphibians.
They have moist,
shiny skin.

clown tree frog

Tree frogs can
be bright colors.

red-eyed tree frog

Tree frogs have two short legs and two long legs. Their feet have toe pads.

orange-legged tree frog

places tree frogs live

Tree frogs live
in tropical rain forests
and other wet places.

emergent layer

canopy layer

understory layer

forest floor

12

Most tree frogs
jump around
the canopy layer
of the rain forest.

They jump from tree to tree.

white's tree frog

Tree frogs hold on to branches with their wide, sticky feet.

dainty green tree frog

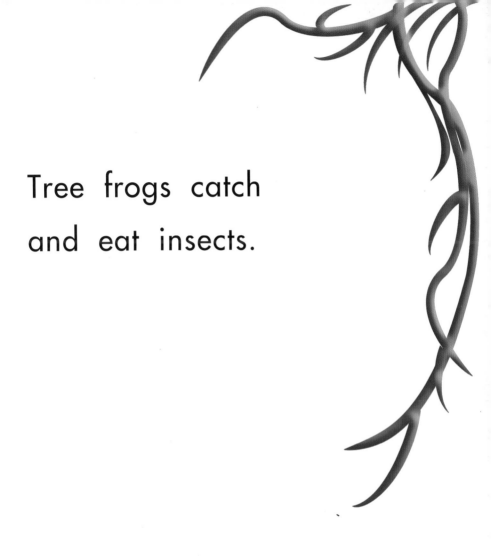

Tree frogs catch
and eat insects.

American tree frog

Tree frogs fold
in their legs
to sleep during
the day.

red-eyed tree frog

Words to Know

amphibian—a cold-blooded animal with a backbone

canopy—the layer of treetops that forms a covering over the forest

insect—a small animal with a hard outer shell, three body parts, and six legs; most insects have two or four wings.

layer—one of the parts of a rain forest; the emergent, canopy, understory, and forest floor are rain forest layers.

moist—slightly wet; moist skin keeps a tree frog cool.

toe pad—a sticky body part on the foot; toe pads help tree frogs hang on to branches and leaves.

tropical rain forest—a dense area of trees where rain falls almost every day

Read More

Baker, Alan. *The Rain Forest.* Look Who Lives In. New York: Peter Bedrick Books, 1999.

Deiters, Erika, and Jim Deiters. *Tree Frogs.* Animals of the Rain Forest. Austin, Texas: Raintree Steck-Vaughn, 2001.

Netherton, John. *Red-Eyed Tree Frogs.* Early Bird Nature Books. Minneapolis: Lerner, 2001.

Internet Sites

The Complete Treefrog Homepage
http://members.core.com/~treefrog

Red-Eyed Tree Frog
http://www.enchantedlearning.com/subjects/amphibians/redeyedtreefrog.shtml

Red-Eyed Tree Frogs
http://artecology.org/redeye.html.html

Index/Word List

Word Count: 87
Early-Intervention Level: 12

Editorial Credits
Sarah Lynn Schuette, editor; Jennifer Schonborn, production designer and interior illustrator; Linda Clavel and Heidi Meyer, cover designers; Kia Bielke, illustrator; Kimberly Danger and Mary Englar, photo researchers

Photo Credits
Bruce Coleman, Inc., 8; Joe McDonald; 4; Jane Burton, 18
Digital Vision, cover, 6, 10, 16
James E. Gerholdt, 1
Visuals Unlimited/Joe McDonald, 14; Larry Kimball, 20

The author thanks the children's section staff at the Allen County Public Library in Fort Wayne, Indiana, for research assistance.